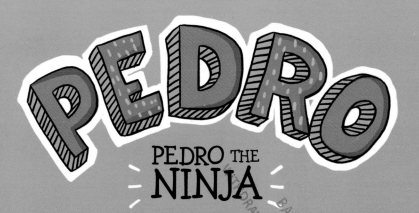

PEDRO THE NINJA

by Fran Manushkin

illustrated by Tammie Lyon

 raintree

a Capstone company — publishers for children

Raintree is an imprint of Capstone Global Library Limited, a company incorporated in England and Wales having its registered office at 264 Banbury Road, Oxford, OX2 7DY – Registered company number: 6695582

www.raintree.co.uk
myorders@raintree.co.uk

Text © Capstone Global Library Limited 2020
The moral rights of the proprietor have been asserted.

Designed by Aruna Rangarajan and Tracy McCabe
Original illustrations © Capstone Global Library Limited 2020
Originated by Capstone Global Library Ltd
Printed and bound in India.

978 1 4747 8964 6 (paperback)

British Library Cataloguing in Publication Data
A full catalogue record for this book is available from the British Library.

Contents

Chapter 1

Karate class

Pedro and Paco were

watching a ninja cartoon.

"Wow!" said Paco. "That

kick was amazing."

"I want to be in a ninja

film," said Pedro.

He yelled, "Hi-YA!"

Oops! Pedro kicked a chair.

"Ouch!" he said. "Being a

ninja is tricky."

"I can help you," said

Pedro's dad. "Would you like

to take karate lessons?"

"Yes, please!" said Pedro.

His dad got Pedro a robe called a *gi.* "Wow!" Pedro said. "I look cool!"

"You do!" said Paco. "I wish I could go to the lesson."

"Maybe next year," said his dad.

JoJo and Katie were in
Pedro's class. Everyone bowed
to the teacher, Sensei Kono.

He said, "The first thing
you will learn is this stance."

Pedro did the stance again

and again.

He told JoJo, "I feel like

a statue."

"But you look fierce,"

said Katie.

At the next lesson, Sensei Kono showed them the side kick. It was tricky. It took balance and lots of practice.

Pedro loved side kicking!

He showed Paco how to do it.

Peppy tried it too. He

kicked over his food bowl.

Chapter 2

Hi-YA!

Every day after

school, Pedro and his

friends pretended they

were in a ninja film.

"Let's practise our kicks," said JoJo.

Oops! She kicked a tree and apples began falling – towards Paco's head!

"Hi-YA!" yelled Pedro,

blocking the apples.

"Cool moves!" said Katie.

"I'm almost a ninja star,"

said Pedro. "It won't be long!"

Punches were the most fun.

Pedro punched beach balls

and balloons.

Pop! Pop! Pop!

No more balloons.

Pedro told Paco, "Ninja stars are always sneaky."

Pedro practised being sneaky by trying to grab cookies before dinner.

"Hi-YA!" yelled his mum.

"Caught you!"

She was sneaky too.

Chapter 3
Ninja stars

Pedro and Paco played ninja

in their room.

"Hi-YA!" Pedro yelled,

jumping out of the cupboard.

Paco screamed and laughed.

"You know," Pedro told Paco, "we are having so much fun, it's okay if we're not ninja film stars."

"Is that so?" said their dad.

The next day, Pedro's friends came over to watch a new ninja film.

"This is a great one," said Pedro's mum.

"I'll say!" His dad winked.

Surprise! The ninjas were Pedro and his friends!

While they were doing karate, Pedro's dad had done some filming. He had been busy making action videos.

"We didn't look very fierce at the start," said Pedro.

"True!" said Katie. "But we got better and better."

"We are the coolest,"

said Pedro.

"We are ninja stars,"

said JoJo.

"Hi-YA!" they yelled.

And they all took a bow.

About the Author

Fran Manushkin is the author
of many popular picture books,
including *Happy in Our Skin*; *Baby,
Come Out!*; *Latkes and Applesauce:
A Hanukkah Story*; *The Tushy
Book*; *Big Girl Panties*; and *Big
Boy Underpants*. Fran writes on
her beloved Mac computer in New York, USA,
without the help of her two naughty cats,
Chaim and Goldy.

About the Illustrator

Tammie Lyon began her love of
drawing at a young age while
sitting at the kitchen table with
her dad. She continued her love
of art and eventually attended
the Columbus College of Art
and Design, where she earned
a bachelor's degree in fine art. After a brief
career as a professional ballet dancer, she decided
to devote herself full-time to illustration. Today she
lives with her husband, Lee, in Ohio, USA. Her dogs,
Gus and Dudley, keep her company as she works in
her studio.

Glossary

balance keep steady and not fall over

fierce daring and dangerous

gi judo, karate or tae kwon do uniform

karate martial art using controlled kicks and punches

ninja someone who is highly trained in Japanese martial arts and stealth; in the past, ninjas were often spies

sensei teacher or instructor of martial arts such as karate

sneaky able to move in a secret manner

stance position of a fighter's feet and body

Let's talk

1. The ninja cartoon inspired Pedro to learn karate. What do you think he liked about the cartoon? Has a TV series or book ever inspired you to learn something new? Talk about it!

2. Do you think that Pedro is a good big brother to Paco? Why or why not?

3. At the end, Pedro says that the kids were not fierce ninjas at first, but Katie points out that they got better and better. Explain what they did to get better at karate.

Let's write

1. Ninjas are described as fierce in this story. What else might be described as fierce? Make a list of five or more ideas.

2. Imagine that Pedro really was a ninja film star. What would his film be called? What would it be about?

3. Write down three facts about karate or ninjas. If you can't think of three, ask a grown-up to help you find some in a book or on the internet.

★ Why did the ninja go to
  university?
  She wanted to be a NINJA-neer.

★ What do ninjas say when they
  see you?
  "Hi-YA!"

★ What do ninjas drink
  during the summer?
  iced kara-TEA

★ What is the ninja's favourite seafood?
swordfish

★ What was the ninja told after a job interview?
"You're hiya-d!"

★ What rugby position do ninjas like most?
kicker

THE FUN DOESN'T STOP HERE!

Discover more stories and characters at

www.raintree.co.uk